ANGELS WITH DIRTY FACES

Kevin James

Published by New Generation Publishing in 2019

Copyright © Kevin James 2019

First Edition

The author asserts the moral right under the Copyright, Designs and Patents Act 1988 to be identified as the author of this work.

All Rights reserved. No part of this publication may be reproduced, stored in a retrieval system or transmitted, in any form or by any means without the prior consent of the author, nor be otherwise circulated in any form of binding or cover other than that which it is published and without a similar condition being imposed on the subsequent purchaser.

ISBN: 978-1-78955-634-6

www.newgeneration-publishing.com

New Generation Publishing

Preface

I want to cast your mind back to a rather distant Swinging Sixties to give you a feel for the atmosphere of that era. Usually summers were hot, The Beatles led the way in music, Carnaby Street a world leader in fashion, black and white television, phone booths with penny slots. The environment in this village was pleasant enough for the majority were, as we say, quite well to do. Whereas the four young lads were always nearly skint. The main objective was to grab any work such as gardening, cleaning cars, tidying up the church, hay-making, sticking up skittle pins, as long as they could up to Friday, then they would go to a sea side resort and have fun and a meal as a treat for themselves. It was their form of escapism though the village was quite picturesque with the old church halfway up the hill and surrounding woods, orchards and fields, they would feel trapped in this mundane quiet life. There was hardly any traffic, or street lights. It was boredom (when work was scarce) that would be followed by mischief or pranks. They never stayed home much as their parents told them to get out from under their feet at an early age with soft words of encouragement. They would cancel out frustration by getting together in a hayrick, that was hard to find on a wet day, playing cards, consuming smuggled cider and food an adult had bought at the village stores. I hope this is an insight to those angels with dirty faces.

Contents

		Pages	
Part 1	Scrumping and the Plum Award	1	Something in the Air (Thunderclap Newton)
Part 2	Grounded in the Garden and Lane	5	With a little help from my friends (Joe Cocker)
Part 3	Blackberrying	8	Blackberry Way (The Move)
Part 4	Stripping Ivy and her dead wood	11	Poison Ivy (The Coasters)
Part 5	Jumble Sale	14	Good Vibrations (Beach Boys)
Part 6	A take-away after tea	18	Return to Sender (Elvis Presley)
Part 7	Sledging	22	Whiter Shade of Pale (Procol Harum)
Part 8	Vicar Remembers fete day	25	Crying in the Chapel (Elvis Presley)
Part 9	Saturday visit to town	29	Ticket to Ride (Beatles)
Part 10	Great Escape on a Winter's Day	33	Smoke Gets in your eyes (The Platters)
Part 11	A bad day on Good Friday	37	Friday on my mind (The Easybeats)
Part 12	Just another Saturday	41	Devil in Disguise (Elvis Presley)

Part 1 – Scrumping and the Plum Reward

It was a typical quiet day in late Summer when the little Angels - Wookey, Bookie, Cookie and Rookie decided to meet up, and between them their plan was to use the public footpath which passed below the woods. One third of the way down from the top was an orchard, going down towards the back gardens of houses and farm buildings.

They met at the corner of the lane where Wookey gathered his troops, Bookie, Rookie and Cookie, to ask if they had a bag each for their spoils; if they got lucky of course. Cookie would have his bag of course, it was dead certain that <u>he</u> would!! Bookie and Rookie were asked to leave their radio at home as Wookey said the only thing they all needed was a wooden club which they would obtain from the ravine by the roadside, when going up the hill. Now Cookie was playing up as he wanted some sweets from the local village stores. At last they were on their way to "Hill Lane", stuffing their faces with chews, nougat and portions of broken biscuits. They arrived at the gate and climbed over into the first field where Bookie and Rookie climbed the Milk Churn Stand to investigate if any milk was in them.

Of course there was no milk!! Cookie was too involved in chewing nougat to take notice!

As they got into the first field they collected as many flattish stones as possible, because further up the field was a small pond that the cattle often used for drinking. They were going to play at "skimming". They arrived at the pond and took it in turns at crouching low and shooting the stones across the surface of the pond. Bookie and Rookie were tops at skimming stones that "hopped" several times over the water.

"Now come on!" said Wookey, "We don't want to run short of time. We must go to the ravine and carve ourselves a club from the branches that grow there." Each of them carried a pen knife. The club was needed to bash brambles that usually covered the footpath at certain points.

Due to the heat and being a bit edgy, one of the lads decided to take off his top and tie it round his waist. They were now approaching the first three bar fence. The sun was being faded out as the woods came into sight; it was eerie and very quiet and a lot darker. They knew that the first three fields didn't have many apple trees, but a few cattle and sheep roamed around. They sneaked quietly across the next two fields, planning their moves as the cattle and sheep drifted down the fields nearly out of sight. When Bookie, who was on the other twin's shoulders (Rookie's) banged his forehead on a low branch, he soon forgot the pain when he saw the branches sagging with the weight of the apples.

The trouble was, they weren't the only visitors, there were loads of wasps (or they used to say **flies in 'rugby shirts!'**) There were so many apples on the ground they could hardly walk but most of these were eaten by wasps. If only they had a larger stick with a hook! The journey down the field towards the back of the houses, the better the apples and the more risky it got!

When they were just about to turn back, who else but Cookie would notice the jackpot. There it was, a couple of well grown plum trees one in front and one behind a crumbling stone wall. The plums were hanging like grapes, but out of reach. Wookey stood there with his mouth agape, as Bookie, Rookie and Cookie chewed noisily on their scrumping gains. Wookey hushed up his down-beat troops and declared that they should get back for tea and return in the evening. He stated that he had a crafty idea to which they hastily asked, "what's that?" Wookey replied, "wait and see!"

As they were turning to go back up the field, Rookie picked up a golf ball from under his feet. Obviously someone had been practising in their back garden. They were going back a lot quicker than they came, gradually getting closer to the ravine. Wookey halted the lads and explained he needed two six-foot poles for the evening, explaining it was part of his plans.

Eventually Wookey got his poles and they went up the road on the way home, rather than disturb the sheep. Rookie had unravelled the golf ball, which had elastic inside and was spinning it around his head and it was getting further away and going at quite a speed when it suddenly careered towards the road and bounced right back, straight at his forehead!

Now both twins, Bookie and Rookie had lumps on their foreheads! They soon arrived back at the lane where their houses were. After tea they met in Wookey's back garden, where Wookey got an empty can from the rubbish bin and chiselled a 'V' shape in it and nailed it as best he could to one of the poles. He brought some string with him and off they all marched with scrumping gains in their heads. Bookie, Rookie and Cookie all stared at Wookey with admiration but they had to press on and not hang around because it could become difficult to see. Eventually they got to the orchard. Wookey decided it was time to tie the two six-foot poles together to make one long pole. Then they crept down within range of the plum trees. Wookey instructed his troops to be ready to run. It all went to plan as Wookey sent the carved end of the pole up to plums and managed to pick two to three off at a time and deliver them into the grasping hands. Rookie also gave it a go. Wookey had to hush them up as they were so amused on their way back up to the orchard. By now it was getting quite dark.

They were just about to climb over the fence when they heard a loud snorting noise that scared the wits out of them. A horse appeared from behind a bush, which then kept them more alert. They were now close to home at the top of the lane when 'Mr Know-It-All' on the corner said "you should patent that **invention** you have in your hands."

Well about half-an-hour later in the shed, Wookey's father said "What on earth are you painting those poles for?" When Wookey replied "Mr Know-It-All' on the corner said I should paint this idea." Then Wookey's father laughingly said "he meant **patent** your inventions, that means register it so no-one has the right to copy it, not **PAINT** it!!

Part 2 – Grounded in the Garden and Lane

Word got out about the sneaky raid on the plum trees. The boys suspected 'Mr Know-It-All' on the corner. Their fathers were out and had instructed them to dig the garden, even though it was just a small patch, and plant some seeds; in other words learn to be useful! They found that a trowel and spade was what they needed – a trowel for digging the weeds up and a spade to turn the earth over. All four of them were bored after a while. Even the neighbours were saying a prayer for them to clear off and give them some peace! So they decided to go out in the lane, which was a cul-de-sac, with a circle at the bottom where you could have two players opposite each other, to kick a tennis or hard ball to the curb opposite and, if successful, it counted as a goal. After 20-30 visits to neighbours' gardens to fetch the ball, and the ball making marks on a couple of parked cars, it was time for them to go home to have some dinner. After dinner they met again in the gardens, knowing that they had to do some work. They felt down in the dumps when Rookie cracked a joke to cheer them up. He said, "**What do you call two rows of cabbages?**" After a silence and puzzled looks, scratching their heads trying to guess what the answer was, Rookie said, "**A dual cabbage way!**"

Of course Wookey had to respond with a joke, even though they were using up valuable time. "**Here's a joke about a snail**" he said, "A man hears a tap at the back door. He opens the door and sees a snail on the floor and kicks it up the path. **A year later he hears a tap at the back door again. When he opens it the snail looks up at him and says, "What was that for?"**

They get back to digging as Wookey was digging deep (he was the only one keen on gardening) he started to unearth some clay, bluish in colour. They each grabbed a handful and proceeded to mould it into different shapes. When thrown against the house wall they were amused to see it stick to it.

They noticed the runner beans at one end of the garden, supported with cane sticks, and saw there some shorter sticks about 3 feet which brought about a mud slinging match.

They gathered as much clay as they could. It was then agreed there would be two boys at each end of the garden. One end had two old armchairs to hide behind and the other end had the row of runner beans. From then on it was like a battlefield, they knew it was quite dangerous but got such a thrill as the clay balls at the end of the canes came whistling past their ears. The neighbours came out and got their washing in! The boys thought it was only soft clay and couldn't harm anyone. There were clay lumps on some parked cars, on the telegraph poles and even on the walls of the houses opposite! At the other end of the gardens, where the old armchairs were, there was a ditch which had trees protecting it.

This was mischief at its maximum. Sooner or later (and they didn't realise it) there would be a price to pay. Several times one end said "let's stop and tidy up before tea, but the other end couldn't resist attacking again, but all was to stop suddenly when the neighbour opposite, called Bill, stood at his gate pointing to the window, which he said he had been sitting behind, having his tea, when the **mud missile** came through. It obviously had a **stone** among the clay which knocked Bill's boiled egg out of the egg cup! Wookey faced the music with Bill who kindly said he would put the glass in if they paid for the glass. The boys borrowed the money and would pay it back on Saturday when they sold their blackberries. They were lucky that the builder who sold the glass was about on a Sunday morning when returning to the top of the lane, Mr 'Know-It-All' commented, on seeing the glass, "you kids are always a **pain in the rear.**" They then were lectured about how easily one of them cold have got a missile in the eye.

"Never mind," said Mr. 'Know-It-All,' You'll all be selling cow dung by the bucket load as manure for people's roses. He sniggered to himself. They looked puzzled at each other. What could he mean? On approaching the house they heard the cries of cattle in the garden. They had forgotten to shut the garden gate so the cattle had strayed from the field down the lane, only to find their garden gate open; in fact the only one open in the cul-de-sac. Just their bad luck!

Part 3 – Blackberrying (thorn in the side!)

With September, hay-making slowing up, the lads spent the evenings before Saturday morning blackberrying. Joe, who paid the boys, came on Saturday mornings with his blue van and scales to weigh them up. Cookie and Wookey would use Dykes Lane and Bookie and Rookie used Crooked Lane for access to their pickings.

As usual they came home from school, had tea and set out in their separate directions. This was done so they were not all crowding into one area and also to split them up so they could concentrate more on filling their plastic buckets. They didn't have a lot of time because the nights were getting darker but this was their last night so they had to 'go for it.' Wookey and Cookie came across a long narrow field with a hedge down through it dripping with blackberries. Using his hook he was pulling the branches over, with some blackberries almost the size of golf balls. They couldn't believe their luck. They asked themselves why hadn't anyone else been there, it was too good to be true. Their buckets filled up easily. Peering through the hedges as they were picking the berries, Cookie said he could hear the noise of a chain rattling. They both stared intently and all of a sudden they could see a black and white friesian bull scuffing the ground. Wookey reassured Cookie that they had a long thick hedge between them and the gate was at the bottom. Wookey said everything was "Hunky Dory" and they came "sailing along" putting Cookie in a more relaxed mod. Their buckets filled up so quickly so there was no need to go to the whole length of hedge. The rest would keep till next week. They walked away from the hedge towards the gate; they could see that the last twenty to thirty feet cut away so as to let the cows (and the bull) use both fields. They could see the hoof marks embedded in the ground. They then noticed the bull with his sinister length of chain hanging from his nose. Cookie and Wookey stood there for seconds, frozen with fear, as the bull was scuffing the ground, just like a sprinter at the starting gate! They ran for their lives, hanging onto their buckets. They vaulted the gate with blackberries scattered in all directions. It was a close shave. It was a good job that the buckets had filled up easily. They collected all they could and set out to go home.

Not far from the top of their lane they saw Bookie and Rookie looking very shaken and looking as though they had been dragged through a hedge backwards, and they didn't have many blackberries.

Wookey in his leader-some voice asked what had happened. Rookie said than on finishing their picking they couldn't resist going into a certain orchard as the apples there were commonly known as Beauty of Bath and were delicious. When plucking a few apples to fill up their buckets they heard and saw the charge of the farmer coming over the gate at the bottom, angrily waving a stick. They ran across the footbridge into the next field and then the next two fields before the farmer was forced to give up. At the last footbridge, being slightly rotten, it caved in and sent him down to his knees in ditch water.

All four of the boys headed back home with their buckets looking light. When approaching the top of the lane, Mr. 'Know-It-All' said, "What's the point in **eating** most of them? Peering into half empty buckets.

Saturday morning arrived. Wookey and Cookie used to wonder why Bookie and Rookie usually had the same amount of berries but they always weighed more. The reason came to light when Cookie went round earlier than expected and noticed one of them pouring water over the fruit. "Well," they said, "They say a pint of water weighs a pound and a quarter." However, on this occasion they were sharing the total.

Joe turned up in his old blue van and promptly got the scales out and paid the boys by the pound in weight. At midday they did their usual, catching the bus into town, approximately two to three miles away, where they treated themselves to a slap up meal and then proceeded to the amusement arcade where the roulette machine milked them of their last few pennies. They even gambled their bus fares so they started walking home down the dirt track lane, then across the fields. As they travelled it started to rain, then approaching the top of the lane they looked like drowned rates. Mr 'Know-It-All' said "I bet you didn't gamble on the rain coming! Still, it will make the blackberries grow like **pennies from heaven**!!"

Part 4 – Stripping Ivy and her dead wood

It was now early December and the boys Bookie, Rookie, Wookey and Cookie had managed to build the go-karts between them which they used to race down Hill Lane, which came down by the woods. Winter was coming on and the boys sometimes worked in the woods, stripping ivy off the trees for 3d (three pence) Each boy had a different coloured ball of wool to separate one from the other and the three lads were told they could have the dead wood, if they could take it away. Well I expect you could guess what's next.

They were up next morning at 6.30 a.m. armed with one small bow saw and hay bale strong and two go-karts. They had three tasks ahead of them once they got to the top of the hill.

With gloves, balaclavas and tough boots they were quite warm when they reached the top of the hill. There was no real rush but they wanted to get back before some of the neighbours were about.

The first task was to check the field next to the wood for any rabbits that might be caught. None of us like this but rabbits are really nice meat. They never let on but sometimes they let them loose!

It started to snow but luckily they had to go into the woods for the next task. It was quite dark and silent and they had to worry about adders.

They ventured in different directions with their coloured balls of wool. They realised that the thinner the trees the quicker the work and the more money they would get! Not that the boys were trying to pull the wool over the owners eyes! The boys knew that getting the wood down hill and home would, if you like, 'earn some house points,' but realised that other kids in the village didn't need to do what they were doing, so were obviously better off. As each tree was <u>stripped</u> they pulled out any dead wood from the undergrowth. They tried to cut the wood to approximately 6ft to fit the go-kart and loaded the kart up as high as they could so they wouldn't have to come again for quite a while. They had some empty cow-cake bags that they could put the small pieces in. Up to now the boys were quite quiet and kept their heads down and just wanted to get home. The owner appeared and started to count the trees they had cleared but was quick to note that some trees had wool tied in two places, high and low, and was quick to point this out!! She didn't hang around because of the cold. Bookie and Rookie steered one kart and Wookey and Cookie the other, with money rattling in their pockets and heading home, they became very excited. Wookey noticed a tree that had fallen over onto another tree at an angle and he started to run up that tree. It was a challenge he was to regret because not far up the tree he slipped and came down flat on his face, ending up giving his left arm, most certainly, a greenstick fracture.

With the two karts loaded up and a steep hill to get down, each kart was on the opposite side of the road with a part of the kart steered into the mud and loose stone kerbing to help slow the kart. Wookey had to lever with one arm. Luckily this road had hardly any traffic. Eventually the boys got on level ground, out from the trees that shaded them, but were now out in the open and noticed the snow more.

As they got closer to home they saw a few people walking their dogs. They wished they could get some of the wood. Wookey suddenly came up with a brainwave, he said, "How about making a frame together for cutting the long pieces of wood into logs? We could use the empty meal bags to fill them and the karts to deliver them."

Rookie said they would have to search further afield for some wood but Wookey said, with a glint in his eye, "The odd small tree wouldn't be missed if we covered it in mud." He had almost forgotten about the pain in his arm as he and the other lads had 'pound signs' in their eyes!! They had just come around the corner when there was the last person they wanted to see ..

Mr. 'Know-It-All.'

It was almost that he knew they were coming. Even the snow had stopped. "I see you're doing useful work, you have decided to turn over a **new leaf and are branching out in the log trade!**"

Rookie replied "You are barking up the wrong tree," and Mr. 'Know-It-All' walking back up his path turned and giggled as he blurted out "I suppose you have got **log books** for those vehicles?" Rookie was about to holler back when Wookey, in a diplomatic way, said, "Think about it Rookie, the coalman will let him down one day and he might be glad to buy from us."

Rookie replied, "There is certainly no **saw dust** up there in your head! Good thinking!"

Part 5 – The Jumble Sale

Wookey, Bookie, Cookie and Rookie were searching the ditches for empty lemonade bottles which gave a return payment. Anything to get a little cash! They were searching around the back of the Village Hall and noticed the top toilet window open. This gave them the idea that if one of them climbed into the hall, he could open it up for the other three.

Well it so happened that the next day was to be a jumble sale at 2.15 p.m. They noticed people carrying items into the hall and the boys told them they were collecting rubbish for the Guy Fawkes bonfire. It was now quite dark when they went to back and crept up to the back of the hall. Then panic set in as they suddenly realised they were breaking the law! But Bookie said, "If two of you keep a look out the other two can climb up and get in the toilet window."

Wookey reasoned that all of them were desperate for shoes and if they sneaked in they could get a look at the goods before they opened. They decided to toss a coin. They were so nervous and felt like 'turkeys in November.' They tossed the coin again and eventually Wookey and Cookie got in and were scouting through the contents when the main doors opened. The boys ran back to the toilets where they could hear the people walking towards the stairs, leading to where they were. Cookie climbed out and lowered himself down the drain pipe. Wookey got out and was hanging on to the overflow pipe when it snapped and sent him hurtling towards the ground, bumping his chin on his knees. All four of them scarpered across the field. "Never again," said Cookie as each of them trembled.

Wookey said, "There were some good shoes there, at least we know now that it was worth climbing up for."

Saturday afternoon all four of them were outside the hall at least 45 minutes before the main doors opened. They decided to forget their idea of getting in through the toilet window, after all it was very risky and unlawful!

They knew exactly where to head for and each of them bought some shoes. They even won a jar of toffees and also got a set of pram wheels to make another go-kart, also a wooden frame (called a horse) which they knew was idea for resting timber on and for cutting up logs.

On the way out of the hall they took an interest in a box of old LP records. This was going cheap as no-one had taken any interest in it. All the lads were keen to have these because of the fun they going to have; nothing to do with music, that's for sure!

Sunday, it rained most of the day, so it would be Monday evening before they would get to look at the LPs. Monday was a bad day because the boys were embarrassed by the comments of one or two of the girls in the school about their clothes, bought at the weekend sale. This resulted in a slanging match which got the boys barred from the coach for 3 days. There were some fairly wealthy people in the village that they had done gardening for.

Straight from school then home, the boys went out as soon as they could as it was fairly dark. Off they went with their records tied down on the go-kart. In the meantime, unbeknown to the lads, a certain avid record collector had been to the sale too late and was trying to track down the lads to offer them good cash. He finds the lads near the field where each of them were tossing the LPs like boomerangs. They were totally amused at their swing motion, some were soon broken in half, some would swerve to almost return to them. They had one or two close shaves!

They were collecting the debris, all the pieces of records, and putting them in a cow-cake bag. The collector stood nearby, almost in tears. "What have you boys done? I would have offered you at least a tenner for the records! Maybe more!"

"How did you find us?" asked Wookey.

"Well a man leaning on his gate at the top of the lane told me," he replied.

Wookey said, "Well that's about all we need! Roll on the next jumble sale and pray someone puts in a load of records again!" They looked at each other and realised they would have to make their own way to earning money and not just rely on lucky breaks.

They had to head home now and were dreading the thought that Mr 'Know-It-All' would be in his usual corner of the lane, leaning on his gate.

As they came around the corner, there he was. He said loudly, "I hear you boys have had had a **smash hit** in the record business and gone to the **top of the charts** with a record aptly named 'Stupidity.' If he was to offer what he says, you can guarantee they are worth a lot more. And throwing those LPs on a dark night is dangerous."

Wookey said, after listening to Mr. 'Know-It-All', "Don't you ever make mistakes?"

Mr. 'Know-It-All' replied, "The only mistake I have made is **admitting I made a mistake** in the first place. I will probably watch Top of the Pops while you boys will get a hard time from your parents for being naive, but, of course, I had to inform them about the stranger who was the collector to put the record straight!"

Part 6 – A Take away after tea

Christmas was nearly over and everything was rather dull as the lads, Wookey, Cookie, Bookie and Rookie couldn't do any jobs as it was quite wet and some people were away. This was always a good opportunity for some sort of mischief to develop.

Well the lads met on the corner of the lane where Mr 'Know-It-All' was usually parked. Wookey explained how he had watched his Dad, who was desperate for a cigarette, cut some paper and roll up some tea leaves. The lads looked at each other; you could tell that something was brewing in their heads!

They chipped in together for a small packet of tea. Over to the corner store they strolled. The shop keeper was bemused! As they went out of the door, Wookey noticed a lot of empty boxes and an odd roll of Christmas wrapping paper. He asked the shop keeper if they could have the boxes and paper. He sent Cookie home to fetch some sticky tape. Cookie already had some matches on him. It was decided to head for the houses around Hillside Lane, where cattle were kept in some of the barns, but one barn was empty.

Wookey led the way with a mischievous look in his eye, the boys, Bookie, Rookie and Cookie knew that they might be smoking tea but weren't quite sure about the boxes and paper. They went across the fields to the barns, where it was deadly quiet, went into the empty barn and cleared out any loose hay that was there, then they put the small planks of wood that were used as props to keep the door open, across the trough to act as a table. Rookie said, "We have got the tea, paper, tape, matches, but you have got to cut the paper! Luckily I have got a knife with scissors attached." he said with a smirk.

Well production was about to begin. Cookie, cutting the paper, Wookey rolling the would-be cigarette, Bookie sticking a little tape on them. Who of course would be first to try it? Cookie! (As his name suggests he would try most things, especially food!) They rolled up at least three each and decided they would stay in the barn, away from public view. They couldn't help giggling, as it was exciting doing something they thought was naughty. They then promised to keep all this to themselves; it certainly proved to perk up a dull, wet afternoon.

The lads then said to Wookey, "Well tell us what is in that crazy mind of yours?"

"Well," said Wookey, "It is naughty but it will be harmless and for sure we will have a laugh!"

"Well tell us then," said Rookie.

"OK, we will fill each of the five empty cartons with cow muck from the barn next door to us and carefully wrap each carton with some of the wrapping paper and sticky tape."

Everyone burst out laughing at the thought of this prank; two of the lads were almost falling into the manure pile from loss of control in laughing.

They put the cartons into an old cow cake bag so as not to arose suspicion.

They decided to go home, have some tea, then leave again, making out they were going to sing a few Christmas Carols. They couldn't wait! They knew there was a long fence behind which was a thick copse with a house behind. This was an ideal hiding place.

The first of the five parcels was left outside the fence, but easily noticeable. The lads stayed behind the fence, trying not to make a noise. The third motorist who came along skidded to a halt, quickly got out, grabbed the parcel and sped off.

They could see enough between the slats of the fence. Then the second parcel went the same way, which was a little boring for the lads. On the opposite side of the road was a proper footpath. When the coast was clear the third parcel was left there in a casual fashion. Well, out of the blue the well known village gossip appeared on her bicycle. Her eyes nearly popped out on springs and she nearly got run over crossing the road to get to the parcel.

They were all praying that she would open it but they heard her say, "Post Office – that must be lost property!"

They planted the fourth box in hope of a real giggle, then waited anxiously. A familiar cough was heard and who should come along but Mr 'Know-It-All', making for his local pub for a pint of beer. He shoved the box with his walking stick at first, but curiosity got the better of him and he craftily hit it into the hedge opposite to pick up on the way home.

The boys then went further down the road where they climbed up some trees to be well camouflaged so that they had a bird's eye view. They left the last parcel for one last giggle prior to going home, when, in the absolute silence, the motorist stopped and the young girl got out, ran over to the parcel, picked it up and got back in the car.

The lads didn't wish this on anyone but the box opened somehow and the contents were scattered inside the car. The lads were trying to hold their laughter, as they might have given away their position. On the way home they all felt very guilty as they didn't expect that!

The next day the lads were off school as each of them had been sick. They knew it was because they had been smoking the tea. Later as the lads gathered at the top of the lane, Mr 'Know-It-All' commented, "It's strange that all four of you were ill! Well there is no smoke without fire. I expect you lads were **brewing** up some mischief, if the truth was known!" After that they wondered if he had known about their antics. The lads were left thinking, did he pick up the carton from the road?

All of a sudden Mr 'Know-It-All' handed the carton to the lads and said, "You will have to **box** clever to catch me out! I recognised the wrapping paper from the local shop and from a car that called at the pub a man was overheard saying, 'that was some Christmas present,' and he intended to report it!"

"Well I put two and two together and came up with you four urchins getting wrapped up in a prank as usual!"

Part 7 – Sledging

It was a bright snowy morning while the boys waited for the school coach, which seemed to be rather late. Wookey, Cookie, Bookie and Rookie were getting excited as it looked as though they might be having the day off school. This was confirmed by a message to one of the parents. Off home they went to get their dreaded school uniform off, and on with their old togs. They couldn't wait to get up over the hill, go to their secret hideaway hayrick, which was set back in a field, fairly hidden away. They had a few sandwiches and chocolate bars. As they peered out of the hayrick the snow was slowing down. They had one sledge and a couple of trays which were not the greatest things to sledge with.

Wookey suddenly noticed an 8ft x 4ft sheet of corrugated galvanised iron that was lying almost in the ditch but in good condition. It looked better than the sheet on the shed at home in which they cut up their logs. They rushed home to swap the sheets over. At least now they had got rid of the hole in the roof! This sheet would carry all four of the. Wookey said, "We'll have to fold over the sharp edges and also put a fold front and back of about 6 inches to enable the 'sledge' to slide forward instead of biting into the snow.

They set back up the hill using the road that led to the top. It was a terrific sight; people going down the hill on trays, lumps of wood and even car bonnets. The car bonnets were first but they would suddenly spin around at a dangerous speed. Looking down the hill it was a very long slope, which eventually flattened out near the houses. Over to the left was an extension to a grave yard with the mounds of old graves sticking up. Their excitement was building up! The trick was to get on the sheet all together, because there was the possibility of it slipping away.

On the countdown of 3-2-1 off they set. The more they gripped the sides and pulled them up, the faster they went! People before them were rushing out of the way in all directions. It was a fantastic feeling! All of a sudden they collided with a mound of grass, which set them on course for the graveyard, where the fencing had almost disappeared under the snow.

They took off slightly due to the drift and landed not far from two graves. Goodness knows what people were thinking as they stared in disbelief. Then the vicar appeared looking fairly amused when he commented, "You could say you have made a **grave mistake**." They all offered to clean out the church gutters to make up for their intrusion, as they had already done in the past.

Finally they all wanted to have one more go up to the hill. They once again got to the launching point when the snow began to fall again. Off they went, hoping to stop short of the private gardens, but ploughed into bramble bushes. The front two boys were covered in brambles and the two at the back helped to get all the brambles off them. It was now getting dark but still was very beautiful with the snow floating down. To keep dry the obvious thing to do was to turn the sheet over, put it on their heads and away they marched down the road with Wookey steering the way. By the side of the road was a line of conker trees and opposite was a milk church stand. Little did they realise that some of the people sledging weren't happy to scatter out of way and three or four of them were lying in wait with a colossal number of snowballs which they collected when waiting for their prey.

Just as they got in close range, the salvo of snowballs started pelting them and they turned the sheet on its side, like holding a shield, only to get bombarded with another salvo from behind the milk churns. They got more or less soaked, so it was a little bit of revenge, well and truly!! They continued on their way with the sheet back over their heads. They travelled along the road hardly able to see their way due to the folds back ad front. They got close to Mr 'Know-It-All's' neighbour. The lads had had enough by now and scooped up snow from the road surface and threw them back. Unfortunately one of the snowballs must have had a stone in it.

Just their luck, it landed on the greenhouse of Mr 'Know-It-All!' Out of the door, like a shot, he came! That will cost you," he shouted at the boys, "You will pay for that!"

To which they cheekily replied with the old saying, "You have got a snowball's chance in hell!"

"Right," said Mr 'Know-It-All.' marching towards their houses.

Wookey blurted out, "No! No! How about a bag of our logs?"

"Make it two bags and it's a deal," said Mr 'Know-It-All.'

Wookey said, "I don't know!"

"It's a deal," said Mr 'Know-It-All.'

Wookey replied, "I don't know! It's **snow-joke**,' he always seems to have his way! He is as slippery as an eel!"

Part 8 – Vicar Remembers Fete Day

It was a fine day and the lads Wookey, Cookie, Rookie and Bookie met outside the local store. The twins Bookie and Rookie had just washed two or three cars and Wookey and Cookie had clinched a job with the landlord of the village pub. They would clean up in the skittle alley and sweep up the back yard. So they all earnt a few bob and were thinking of buying a few treats in the local shops. It was about eleven o'clock and they were thinking of purchasing some local cider through a friend of theirs who was old enough! Just as the friend came into view, who should step out of the shop but an old friend of theirs – the Vicar!

"I will take you boys up on the offer you made back in the Winter when you all kindly decided to drop into the graveyard extension," he said to them. They didn't have the gear they needed but the Vicar said, "I've got all you need in the Church shed."

Because the Church was built into the hill there was a 'gutter alley' all around it, except on the main entry side.

The Vicar said, "You'll still make it to the fete." They got to the Church and noticed that the gutter at its deepest point was six to seven feet high; which meant shovelling the muck and leaves into old bags and carrying them to the council dump. Every time they went back they found more leaves had blown into the gutters.

Eventually, covered in sweat and dirt the lady who handled the Church money came along and said, "You boys can have a packet of peanuts each, on account, at the Village Stores."

The boys didn't exactly jump up and down with gratitude! Home they went to smarten up. As they headed home, of course you can guess who was there, Mr 'Know-It-All.'

He said, "You boys, you look like someone dragged you from the gutter! Gutter snipes I would say!"

They all quickly got changed and at the fete they paid a small entry fee which served as a numbered raffle ticket for a later draw. They knew they had to get to the skittle area.

One of them could stick up the pins and maybe knock an odd pin or two (**accidentally on purpose**) when the other lads were playing there.

As the alley was on timber supports which, if you craftily stood on them, you could vibrate the alley and cause a pin to fall down!

This would have to be before the local professionals dropped in from the village pub.

When one of the boys achieved a reasonable qualifying score on the skittle alley, they would have a look around the fete at the other attraction, the tombola table, table skittles, throwing darts to cards and passing a line ring along a metal line (and if the ring touched the line there was a loud buzz and so your chance ended!)

There was a sort of 'pillow fight,' two people sat astride a section of telegraph pole and each person tried to knock the others off the pole. There was straw spread underneath to soften the fall.

Their favourite activity was plate smashing, which was over in a corner away from the rest.

They used wooden balls to smash the plates. Of course they weren't bad shots as when they collected bottles from the ditches and hedges, any that had no money back on them were balanced on a field gate and they would throw stones at them (of course the glass had to be cleaned up).

It was almost five o'clock when the fete was over. The boys won top prize at the outdoor skittles and they decided they would like to have a go at getting a qualifying score at the skittles in the next village two miles away, but they didn't have enough cash.

They were all ears when they heard one of the farmers saying he needed to get the hay bales, stacked in the large field, ready for loading next morning.

The boys offered to help and the farmer agreed. So home to tea they went and on with oldest jeans they had and on their bikes within half an hour.

It was very hot and quiet across the hay field. The bales weren't too heavy as there hadn't been any rain lately. Eventually they finished and were paid. They rushed home to smarten up, hoping their parents would allow them to go out at this later time. Luckily one of the parents had a darts match in the same village and felt the boys had deserved the opportunity; at least they were not up to mischief! But alas, when they got to the pub all the 'play-offs' were after ten o'clock. That night was the final night. They needed 14 to qualify and take part in the 'play-offs.' Being quite young they realistically didn't have the experience but they wanted to try! They managed to get some qualifying rounds between them.

10.00 p.m. arrived and the list of names were chalked up ready for the play-offs. Some people had four or five goes. Very gradually they played their cards close to their chest.

Bookie hit 15, with one man to go with two chances to play.

Wookey went on to hit 17, this was a good score (when

considering the maximum is 27 with three balls.) The boys were on cloud nine as they were on splits and the last man came to the alley to play. They couldn't quite see the man as everyone stood in front of them and were obviously bigger than them. (The boys were almost counting the money) On the man's last attempt he hit 9 with two balls and hit the lot down with his third ball, scoring 18 and winning the prize.

When the man came into their sight they were gobsmacked! Who should it be but Mr 'Know-It-All!!' They were bowled over! He said, sniggering to himself, "The next time you are cleaning up the alley in our local I could give you some lessons for a small fee!!"

Part 9 – Saturday Visit to Town

Saturday morning approximately 9.00 a.m. the lads are just back from an early morning blackberry pick; the final top us as this was the morning when Joe would arrive in his dark blue van to pay six pence a pound for them (2.5p new money). The lads were topping up their buckets with more blackberries and water was added before the top-up, which Mr 'Know-It-All' on the corner of the lane had noticed. Well Joe was now turning in to the lane. Wookey said, "Oh crikey, someone's got to talk nicely to Mr 'Know-It-All' to keep his attention away from Joe as he might drop the hint that we were adding water to the blackberries to make them weigh more!"

So Cookie (the greedy one) strolled down to him. The lads skilfully explained to Joe that it had rained yesterday, hence the dampness of the berries. Meanwhile Cookie was on his favourite subject – food. He couldn't resist telling Mr 'Know-It-All' that a certain field in Crooked Lane was where mushrooms were plenty and ready to be plucked.

Now all the lads had in their minds was catching the midday bus into the local town, Burnham.

They went home and got changed and smartened themselves up. They met just around the corner from Mr 'Know-It-All's' perch. Cookie was now receiving thanks from the others for keeping you know who out of the way of Joe. Cookie added, "Don't forget Joe said he would buy mushrooms if we found enough."

There on the bus stop almost opposite the village stores they waited for The Green Snake as it was jokingly known. Round the bend it came and Cookie said, "It looks very full." Once inside and sitting they could see that the Bus Conductor was working flat out and was rather confused. So Cookie and Bookie, who took the last two seats, picked up a couple of used tickets off the floor and stuck them in the top pockets of their shirts so the Conductor would see them and think he had already issued them tickets. Well, their trickery paid off this time, as long as a Bus Inspector didn't get on at some point on the journey!

The lads got off at Pier Street and marched down the High Street having a look around Woolworths and the Record Shop and a glance at the clothes in Harry Parry's shop. On the way back up High Street towards Pier Street they headed towards their favourite cafe, The Galley, as it was known. Once inside they ordered egg and chips. Staring out the window whilst eating their meal they noticed a large column of motorbikes making quite a row. The riders were wearing black leather jackets and white silk scarves. Those noisy intruders were commonly known as 'Rockers.' The lads were especially fascinated by their bikes.

They finished their dinner and what better? The next stop on a hot day? The Ice Cream department at Roymar's Shop. They each had one before their trek up to the sea front to visit the Amusement Arcade. On their way to the arcade they checked their money which by now had thinned out a little. But of course in their heads they were going to win some, after all that was the idea! Cookie and Bookie concentrated on the roulette wheel, where the ball could land on various colours, White = 12, Yellow = 6, Green = 4, Red or Black = 2.

Rookie and Wookey were on the horse racing machine with greater values to be won. But they lost all their money, bus fares and all. The prospect of a long walk home was ahead of them. Every time they visited the Arcade they lost their money and had to walk home!! So the lads started to walk towards the outskirts of Burnham and called in at the park. They would have liked to play 'Pitch and Putt' but obviously no money, no game!!

The lads started to make headway towards the lane that would lead them to the rough track where only tractors travelled. There was a ditch either side of the track. Eventually they came to the tarmac of 'Crooked Lane.' Wookey said, "How about, while in this spot we go and pick mushrooms? We can always make a few bob by selling them to Joe the Blackberry man or the local Village Stores?"

As they approached the turn off they noticed a figure of a man disappearing over the bridge. They thought it was probably a pond fisherman. So onwards they marched across two fields to get to the secret spot, only to find lots of stalks left with not a mushroom in sight!! To add to their dismay it started to rain. If they hadn't stopped they could have got home before the rain started. Eventually they got to the village road and, approaching the home bend, a voice rang out with a touch of sarcasm.

"You boys come home in style, you obviously couldn't

go on the bus because your winnings would probably **exceed the weight limit,**" chuckled Mr 'Know-It-All.'

"Very funny," said Wookey.

"Well," said Mr 'Know-It-All' "You are all skint, wet and missed your tea. Oh, on the subject of tea I must go in. I have got a lovely piece of steak and some fresh field mushrooms. I picked them down Crooked Lane."

"You crafty old geyser you," muttered Wookey.

Mr 'Know-It-All' said "Save me buying them at the shops. I will probably sell what's over of course after my meal. I couldn't find **mushroom** in the bag for anyone else!!"

Wookey told his mother about this during the evening. She said, "Sometimes you have got to strike while the iron's hot – in other words you should have gone to get those mushrooms earlier in the day."

Another difficult lesson to be learnt!

Part 10 – Great Escape on a Winters Day

The lads weren't off springs of 'well-to-do' parents. They would have to miss the school trips here and there because money was scarce. They told their parents they didn't mind as long as one day they could 'do a deal,' such as if the weather got bad and the school coach couldn't turn up, then it would be alright for them to have midday onwards up over the hill and wood and so have their own day out. This was agreed by their parents as long as they knew their whereabouts.

As the winter became more severe the lads anticipated that their 'camp night' was getting near. So they went to the local jumble sale at the Village Hall and bought some cooking gear such as frying pan, saucepan and plates, also old lighter sticks. Other items, such as lard, sausages, bread, bacon and even mushrooms would be obtained from the village store.

This particular night the weather turned pretty bad; this was the start of one of the worst winters of that period in the sixties.

Usually the lads came out of their garden gates at the same time. Two of them still wore shorts and the other two grey trousers with blue and grey long socks and white or grey shirts. They were supposed to wear hats but they usually were conveniently lost! They had to pass Mr 'Know-It-All' on the way to the coach stop; it was starting to flicker with snow and the lads were now getting excited. They were all smiles when Mr 'Know-It-All' made a comment. "You all appear to be just little angels but with dirty faces!! An air of peace descends on us as soon as you boys get on that coach." They each huddled under the trees at the stop, praying that the coach wouldn't come.

Twenty more minutes passed. They were now freezing but excited, when a message came through to one of the parents that the coach had broken down. The lads scuppered home as fast as lightening to get their gear on which could handle the weather. The snow was getting thicker as they hurried to the Village Stores to get their supplies. First they carved a club which was good for bashing any brambles that got in the way. They were delayed a little as one or two villagers wanted shopping or to have have their driveways cleared, but this was OK as the cash was handy.

After a snack at midday they started marching up Hill Lane. Their destination for the afternoon was a hayrick, set back off Hill Lane, halfway down a field which was handy for them because the farmer and the public couldn't trudge out there in these conditions. The hayrick was up on the hill top, quite a distance away. All the lads felt good that this was Friday. No school tomorrow!!

They had even managed to bring a bottle of cider!!

Everything was 'Hunky Dory' as they would say. As they climbed up Hill Lane, it felt warmer because the trees hung over the road. When they got to the top they were out in the open and the blizzard seemed worse up there but they hadn't far to go before the hayrick was in sight. They decided to walk close to the hedge so as not to leave footprints to show where they had gone. The hayrick backed out onto the hedge and the boys knew from hay making and building a rick that there was always space at the top.

All they had to do was climb the side that backed onto the hedge and stuff a few bales a bit higher. If the snow started to blow inside they could stack the bales up to it which would allow them to scale down inside for protection and warmth.

They decided to stay until at least 7.00 p.m. and then move onto a field or two away.

This hayrick was their nest for the next few hours. They could climb up inside and spy between the bales and view in the distance the lane which connected the two villages. Hardly a soul was seen as they played cards, comped biscuits and sweets and supped cups of cider which they had planned to have around the camp fire. It was bliss. No Mr 'Know-It-All' and no parents!!

It was so peaceful, just the odd rabbit searching for food. Everything seemed so different at night compared to their daytime exploits in this area. A the evening progressed it was such a beautiful sight across the fields and nature left its own tapestry of designs on the hedges and trees.

One of the lads looked at his beloved Ingersoll pocket watch and said, "Well it's about time we got out of here now and looked for a camp site."

They climbed up behind them because they might not get the chance to do it again. They started walking towards the reservoir that overlooked the village. Leading up to this was a dry ditch with trees and bushes growing on the edge. This made a hallow they could get down into. They would be sheltered by the bushes and they had their club to bash any brambles that might be there.

They searched for some pieces of dried wood and eventually they were all tucked down in the ditch. They had a lighter to get the fire going and with a few rotten sticks and pieces of paper they had brought, they soon had a fire going.

The only trouble was that they were getting a bit bored and irritable with each other. So they then got out the cooking gear and started doing a fry up and dishing out some more cider, which was starting to make them 'throw caution to the winds' as they say!!

Wookey took control. The last thing he wanted was the fire engine trying to get them!! The other lads felt that the cider was affecting them but realised they had to be careful. They said they would be back by 11.00 p.m. but as it approached ten they were beginning to miss their home comforts. They were getting very jittery, seeing odd movements in the bushes as the wind was getting up. Their bravery lasted a bit longer due to finishing the cider, but they thought they had best make headway for home. On of the lads, Rookie, wanted to hang on a bit longer as he had secretly put some chestnuts in the fire to roast. Several more minutes later passed when there was an almighty BANG. Lots of ash was sent flying into the air; they wiped their eyes and looked stunned. Rookie noticed a big red circle in the top pockets of Wookey's coat. He didn't realise that a burning ember had landed in his top pocket!! It looked like a red sun!! Rookie kept very quiet after this incidence!! They covered over the ashes with earth and stones and were on their way home weary and contented.

As they approached the usual corner of Mr 'Know-It-All' he was just back from the Village Pub. When he was Wookey he couldn't resist saying, "Money always seems to burn a hole in your pocket!! Now you are all back I can rest in peace not expecting the woods to be alight!!

Rookie kept quiet about the chestnuts. He was only trying to give a surprise to his mates and anyway, 'it could have been worse.'

Part 11 – A Bad Day on Good Friday

It was expected to be a lovely warm day so Wookey, Cookie, Bookie and Rookie were up and about planning their day ahead as this was the day that the tradition was to walk up the Knoll and have a picnic at the top.

There was one snag and that was money! (or lack of it!) They knew that the Village Store only opened for one hour at midday so they decided that Rookie and Cookie would go the local pub and tidy up the skittle alley after the previous night's competition and Wookey and Bookie headed up the village to Mr. Grant's house whereas she had said to them the previous week she had some wild grass and weeds to be hacked down.

Sure enough Mrs. Grant was there and opened the door. She said she was just on her way out to walk her dog but as they were there she would show them what she wanted them to do. She went out to the shed and brought out two cutting tools known as a Swing King Cutter. She then showed the two lads all around the garden and explained what was what and made a point of mentioning a special shrub she had nurtured to its present height of five feet; a beautiful shrub but frail looking. Mrs. Grant said she would be back in about an hour; she felt that the job should be finished by then. Off she went and Wookey and Bookie decided that would work separately as it would be safer.

As they ploughed into their work they could hear a transmitter radio churning out sixties hits. They were now sweating profusely and, being a little weary, decided to sit in the shed and cool down. They noticed that in there were bottles of home-made wine. There were a lot of bottles so they decided that just a little swig from each bottle wouldn't be missed.

They looked at the little Ingersoll pocket watch and realised they had only ten minutes left. So, to the tune playing next door, 'House of the Rising Sun,' they both worked like beavers, when only final swipe accidentally felled the precious shrub. It fell down with such precision that they knew they had to fix it somehow. So, very carefully they propped the shrub up using twigs entwined in its branches, carefully covering the cut with grass. They both knew that the wine was at the root of the problem!! They could hear the owner coming back with her dog, which was panting loudly. She noticed that everything looked good as she put her dog in the house.

She ambled out of the house, carefully scanning the garden and approached the lads. She sighed and said, "Well everything looks in order!!" She did moan a little about the radio being on. She opened her purse just as a breeze sprang up and to the horror of Wookey and Bookie the special shrub Mrs. Grant was nurturing came crashing down almost across her feet.

She snapped her purse shut and yelled, "Out of my garden!"

Well as the lads were leaving how apt it was to hear the words from another record playing next door, "You had better **go now; go now**!!"

On the way back to meet Rookie and Cookie they searched the hedges for discarded bottles knowing there was a refund on the empties. There were always a few as some people had already been up the hill and back and tended to be not very litter tidy.

They met at the stores and bought the usual crisps and biscuits etc. They were wearing T-shirts but when one got to the top there was usually a cool breeze. There were two ways to access the knoll; one way was the footpath through the church yard and through two large fields to the top. This was usually the safest way and the route families usually went.

The lads voted for Hill Lane; this was mainly road leading to a steep rise through one large field. This was their preferred route; they would pass their favourite conker tree and sometimes the lady in the large manor house might have a small job for them. There was always the chance of a little more cash!!

Sometimes when they were close to the garden, if she was about, they would cheekily ask her for a job. It was decided that later in the evening they would all meet in Hill Lane with their go-karts and have some runs.

Their go-karts had been made from old pram wheels and various bits of wood. Once at the top of the road they followed the old footpath that linked up with a long field to the summit, they more or less passed through a farm yard on their journey.

That first climb was the toughest. By now there were two to three dozen people heading for the top. Once through the swing gate it was a little easier as there were steps cut into the ground. Eventually, when the boys arrived at the summit, they knew that the top dropped down about six feet or so just a bit like an extinct volcano. This allowed them to rest away from the wind. They spent the next two hours just looking at the view with some borrowed binoculars and munching on their crisps and biscuits. Two of them played cards while the other two dug into the earth a bit, hoping to find fossils.

It was decided to go at about 4.00 p.m. and try to get out about 5.30 p.m. with their go-karts.

Finally they got home, had their tea and met at the top of the lane with two go-karts.

There turned out to be three other karts from challengers in the village. While they were up the knoll word had got around about their plan.

Mr 'Know-It-All' was casting his eyes on all the kids and karts. He said, "Five karts? Use your head for goodness sake! You need someone at the bottom, near the finishing line, to stop the traffic!"

The boys scrambled away from him. They were cornered! He would take over and referee the races! They got up to Hill Lane. Five karts each decorated with a fancy name.

All five were lined up across the road. Looking down from the top there was a ditch on the left and an embankment on the right where the woods grew close to the edge of the road. Wookey and Cookie in one kart and Bookie and Rookie in the other. The look-out at the bottom blew a whistle and all five karts shot away. They were neck and neck and came to a slight bend in the road. Wookey's kart shot up the side embankment and sent him head first into a puddle! As he lifted his head he saw blood dripping into the puddle. He sort of panicked as one of the other riders threw him an old towel used for keeping the seat dry. They wrapped the towel around his head and marched back towards home, pulling their kart behind them. At the bend (what luck) Mr 'Know-It-All' said, "**I know I said use your head but that's ridiculous!**"

As they ignored him, hurriedly heading towards home, they could hear Mr 'Know-It-All' saying, "I suppose you've all **thrown the towel in!**"

Part 12 – Just Another Saturday

Wookey, Bookie, Cookie and Rookie were now in a situation where their bicycles were getting a little rough and they had seen some second-hand bikes they liked, but it was money they needed! And they needed it very soon as someone might beat them to it! They had managed to get a Saturday morning job, each of them, working for two to three hours for aged residents living in the village with premises quite large compared to others. They would often go blackberrying at 7.00 a.m. back at 9.00 a.m. to sell them to Joe with his blue van, who usually arrived around 9.30 a.m. So at 10.00 a.m. they would go to their different places of work. Wookey's job was for an elderly couple; he'd been a commander in the Navy.

Wookey normally worked for 2 and a half hours. First of all he would sweep up, then do a small patch of weeding. During this period the commander – the boss – would emerge out of his beloved room after his regular ritual of listening to the shipping forecast, smoking a Senior Service cigarette, which he held delicately between his long fingers. He would draw a breath and issue the command for the mower to be brought into action. During the next hour of pushing the mower there would be a half-way break. The grass cutting ceased as the commander, with military precision, shouted "Tea!"

Wookey would then go into the kitchen area where he would find biscuits and cake all laid out on a silvery tray. Wookey felt quite an important person! There was only one snag; sometimes the commander's wife would put seedy cake on the tray. Wookey detested that and would secretly hide it in the mower's grass-box! He didn't have the heart to tell them as he loved everything else. The main thing with the commander was that he would always find work for Wookey to do, even during wintry days, such as cutting up various chunks of coal with a sort of 'ice-pick.' The commander always had a military outlook; he was firm but fair.

The afternoon was usually spent in the nearby town but, of course, they were saving their pennies so they decided they would walk round to Hill Lane where four beautiful conker trees were close to the roadside. There were a few youngsters struggling to knock the conkers out of the trees. Being older, they had more physical strength to throw up the lumps of wood. They had to time this carefully as the odd car passed by and they had to make sure they weren't underneath the thrown missiles. Even a horse went by as it seemed one large bunch of conkers were impossible to dislodge. Wookey, being the strongest, thought he would give it one last fling! With all his might he threw a large chunk of wood up, when all of a sudden a familiar voice rang out over the fence by the roadside. Mr 'Know-It-All' couldn't contain his laughter.

Wookey said sharply, "What do you want?"

Mr 'Know-It-All' said, "First of all I would like to congratulate you on learning another lesson on the Law of Gravity; what goes up has to come down! But in your case not an apple! Also I realise you're looking for work, well the Inn 1 and a half miles away are desperate for people to stick up the skittle pins – or so I am told."

Wookey, rubbing his head did thank him reluctantly.

Just as Mr 'Know-It-All' left, the lady who lived not far from the conker trees came walking by with her dog. This lady often asked the boys to do odd jobs and she'd heard the noise of them trying to knock conkers down. She asked them if they would like to earn a few shillings. Two hours were almost all the time they could spare if they planned to go to the Inn.

They marched to the mansion overlooking the village and the lady owner led them to a massive lawn. The lads were a little bemused because it looked like it had not long been cut. Then she pointed out the weeds that were entangled in the grass. She then introduced them to a special rake shaped like a fan with a lot of prongs that were thin and close together.

The lady marked out sections; each of them had one of these rakes and for the next hour or so they all scratched away. They wee easily observed and very hot. They had no shelter, but for a few extra shillings they joked amongst themselves and thought it was similar conditions to a chain gang!

On the way back for tea they contacted the public house confirming that they were available, but it seemed only two of them was required. Wookey said Rookie and Cookie could have a go at the skittles competition later on and if they qualified maybe they could win the prize with Wookey and Bookie sticking up the skittles it was pretty sure they would be close. Wookey commented on this with a real glint in his eye! Bookie reminded Wookey that it was a year ago, on that very skittle alley, that Mr 'Know-It-All' tricked them and took the prize at the last minute.

They arrived at the Pub and put their bicycles around the back. Wookey was concerned that he had no lights and the brakes were not that good, but the show must go on!! Most people were in fancy dress as there was a birthday party coinciding with the skittle match. Well, 10.00 p.m. was the deadline for the 'play-offs.' To be in this you needed 15 or more. As planned Rookie and Cookie turned up to play and when they played they noticed someone staring intently at the alley. He was disguised as a Policeman! When they played a few times the policeman started to walk down towards them.

Wookey blurted out about his bicycle having the defects (He and Bookie were occupied with putting the skittles back in their place, you remember!)

"I am not interested in your bike," said the policeman. "I am just wondering why the pins in the alley seem closer when your two buddies are playing?" Wookey nearly choked, when something told him that behind the disguise was a **slimy voice he recognised**. Mr 'Know-It-All' couldn't help revealing himself, as the lads looked very serious!

Wookey said to him, "Don't you every give up?"

To which he said, "I like to see fair play."

Mr 'Know-It-All' won the skittle match at the end of the night and as the lads were leaving he said to them, "You have to remember, I play in the league whereas you boys, like the grass you told me you raked over, you have just been **scratching the surface and you are rather green!"**

He always seemed to have the last word!!